Identity Theft 101

LIANA BROOKS

OTHER WORKS

ALL I WANT FOR CHRISTMAS

All I Want For Christmas Is A Reaper
All I Want For Christmas Is A Werewolf

FLEET OF MALIK

Bodies In Motion
Change of Momentum

HEROES AND VILLAINS

Even Villains Fall In Love
Even Villains Go To The Movies
Even Villains Have Interns
Even Villains Play The Hero (books 1 – 3 omnibus)
The Polar Terror

TIME AND SHADOWS

The Day Before
Convergence Point
Decoherence

SHORTER WORKS

Fey Lights
Prime Sensations
Darkness and Good

Find other works by the author at
www.lianabrooks.com

Identity Theft 101

INKLET #98

LIANA BROOKS

Inkprint
PRESS
www.inkprintpress.com

Print ISBN: 978-1-922434-48-7
eBook ISBN: 9798215734407

www.inkprintpress.com

National Library of Australia Cataloguing-in-Publication Data
Brooks, Liana 1982 –
Identity Theft 101
42 p.
ISBN: 978-1-922434-48-7
Inkprint Press, Canberra, Australia
1. Fiction—Fantasy—Urban 2. Fiction—Fantasy—
Contemporary 3. Fiction—Short Stories

First Print Edition: January 2023
Cover photo © Lelani38 via Pixabay
Cover design © Inkprint Press
Interior art © Amy Laurens

IDENTITY THEFT 101

Being immortal in the modern world is... tricky.

I really didn't see computers coming. Or the cameras. Or internet.

Odd's blood, but do you know how wild the idea of the internet is when you've spent centuries happily ignoring the gossip about you?

It's like the nosiest old auntie of the land was given the gift of being everywhere at once.

...All right, gift is the wrong word. That would definitely be a curse.

Either way, being immortal has become exceptionally more difficult in the past half century. It used to be as easy as moving mid-plague, or falling down in a battle and staying there for a few hours. Then you'd hike for a few days until you were in a new area and claim you were attacked by robbers, or bandits, or Crusaders, or whoever the local igglywaffin was.

Now there are passports, digital phones, and internet.

And doctors.

Such annoying doctors.

I sat on the cold, paper-covered medical altar looking like a sacrifice to a possibly addled elder-god as a young man only in his sixth decade of life poked at my back with all the grace of enraged hippo.

"This is interesting." A cold-but-youthful finger traced a scar that bisected my back right side. "What happened here?"

"It was years ago." The 1860's maybe? Or was that 1730's? It all blends together after a century or two. I'm fairly certain it was the scar left by a well-sharpened cutlass. Fairly certain. I'd been attacked in the same place in Cairo a century or two before that.

You do tend to remember the first time someone tries to take your lungs out by force. It's... ah... unsettling... not knowing if the strange force that keeps you alive will work against a new kind of injury.

It does.

My head can be crushed. I can be set on fire. I have donated over sixteen kidneys. Eventually, the scar tissue heals and my body regenerates.

I age when I'm badly injured. But it will gradually fade over the next century or so and leave me looking in that middling period of life, not still youthful but not yet old. And I really can't consider myself in my prime when my age is divisible by so many numbers.

Ah ha. Just my little joke.

The doctor gave another poke. "What happened here?"

"Slipped and fell on some farm equipment back in the day." A scythe in the arms of an enraged farmer? Sure that sounded probable. I still think it was a cutlass but that would be hard to explain.

"Where'd you grow up?" the doctor continued the chatter as he looked for the damage from the car accident that had brought me in.

"Out west, mostly." Between gold rushes and dot com booms. I bought property in Aspen when it was cheap. Hong Kong too. And Italy, although I haven't been back since that bratty little painter from Modena put me in a picture of the three wise man visiting Bethlehem.

It's a terrible painting, by the way. The camels look like dragons at a glance and I'm wearing the most obnoxious green-and-star-spangled muumuu. But he got my pointy chin and slightly androgynous features right. The hat, on the other hand, is such an obviously modern affection (*was* a modern affection?) that I nearly laughed myself out of the viewing. I didn't because the food was passable. But within half a century I still had people pestering me about the dang painting.

It was easier to move on.

The doctor patted my shoulder. "No pain anywhere? Full range of motion?"

I obligingly wiggled in the green-striped hospital gown. My shoulders rolled with barely a pinch. My legs were the best they'd been since the 1600's. My back whined in agony but I'm fairly certain that was modernity, not injury. Computers again. Alack and alas.

"I feel great." It was almost not a lie.

The doctor shook his head and blinked. "Not sure how that happened. Everyone else in the wreck has something broken."

One fatality too, but the doctor wouldn't say that until he spoke to the next of kin.

"My car has the best safety rating on the market." I smiled.

"They used the jaws of life to get you out," the doctor said. "Your car is probably totaled."

I sighed, hoping I looked shocked by this news. Cars last ten years, maybe a little longer if you're a careful driver. Horses last at least twenty, and feet will last you forever as long as you keep them warm and dry. "I liked that car."

A complete and total lie. It was ugly, slow, and boring.

The doctor smiled kindly. "Caught in the middle of a six-car pile-up because the lights didn't work? I doubt the insurance is going to argue it's your fault."

"True." The city lights were what had injured my back. Do you know how long it takes to figure out how to rewire and recode the busiest inter-section in the city? So long.

SOOOOOOOOOOOO LOOOOOOONNNNNNNGGGGGG.

I rolled my neck and stretched just thinking about it. Maybe it was time to find one of those tech-free communes for a little while. Go be Amish or hipster or Alaskan for a bit. Although most of Alaska has cellphones and internet these days. The Yukon would be better. It's hard to get a signal in the mountains.

The doctor smiled in easy cama-raderie. "I'll have a nurse bring the dis-charge papers."

"Great, can I get dressed in something?"

"Can family or friends bring you some new clothes?"

The ambulance team had cut off what I'd been wearing.

I winced. "I'm new to the area. This was my first day in the new job."

"I'll have someone bring you a spare set of sweats," the doctor said.

Twenty minutes later I'd signed the paperwork with an illegible scrawl and artfully dripped a bit of water on the corner where my name and alleged birth date went. The nurse was frazzled and rushing between a small child with a high fever, a patient in cardiac arrest, and the other victims of the car crash. By the time anyone noticed the name on the paperwork was washed away, I would be long gone.

"Your things, monsieur." The nurse handed me the broken watch and a black, leather wallet that had taken me ages to find.

I flipped it open and double-checked everything was in good order. Then, on my way out, I *accidentally* lifted a white lab coat with someone's name tag as the ER doc took a quick power nap in a dark room.

Please appreciate how clever I am. It took four months of patient lurking at odd hours to find the doctor's routine and then find an intersection that was busy enough, at the right hour, to pull off the kind of semi-tragic accident that I needed.

In the doctor's coat, I sauntered down the empty after-dark halls of the hospital, cloaked in authority and shadows, and entered the morgue.

The deceased's belongings sat in a cubby with the words DECELLES AC-CIDENT scrawled in a wide hand.

With a gloved hand (curse modern fingerprinting) I pulled the basket out and looked at a matching watch and

wallet of—I flipped his wallet open—
Henri Ruemare.

"Really?" I looked at the deceased.
"That is not the name you were born
with and we both know it."

Brian Seahome, aka Ryan Seastreet,
aka Bryan Street, aka Ren Street, aka
Lamont Funaire (a bit of original
thought on the part of the black market passport creator), aka Henri Ruemare didn't respond.

The Toronto-born, Arizona-raised
menace to society had used his dual
nationality to avoid all kinds of
trouble. Justice for his crimes would
mean a life or two in prison. I spared
the tax payers the burden of keeping
him alive because Brian—excuse me—
Henri, so rude of me to use an old
name—had a one-way ticket to Flor-
ida, and no one who would care if he
died.

The wallet I'd worked so hard to
find dropped into the cubby, effect-

ively ending one life as I picked up a new one.

Henri...

You know, I don't hate the name.

I think I'll wear it for awhile.

THE MAKING OF
IDENTITY THEFT 101

This is another short story in the long line of LIANA WRITES ABOUT IMMORTALS.

What is my obsession? Why do I like writing about the daily travails of immortals? I don't have a good answer for that.

However, I am fascinated by how easy it used to be to reinvent oneself. You move across a continent, or even just across a busy city, and you could make yourself into a whole new person. A tempting idea, I'm sure.

But much harder to execute in this day and age of technological surveillance, AI on smartphones, and well-funded government programs meant to track criminals.

Still... Harder doesn't mean impossible. So why not make a story of it?

Read more by Liana Brooks!

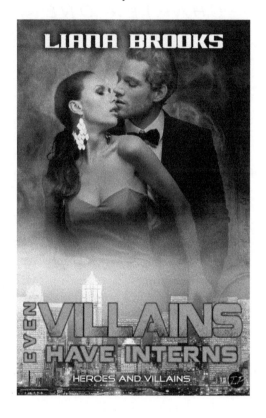

EVEN VILLAINS
HAVE INTERNS
CHAPTER ONE

December 2033

Dear Dad,

Just because Mom mentioned she liked Claude Monet's Grand Canal painting does not mean she wants a copy of it for the house. I know it doesn't mean she wants the original. And telling me not to steal the piece while it's on tour at the Art Institute here in Chicago is not going to convince me to pick it up in time for Christmas. Reverse psychology stopped working when I was twelve.

In other news, you will be happy to learn that Peter Manigault, as painted by Allen Ramsay, mysteriously appeared at the Art Institute this weekend. The curator was very surprised. Personally, I think his shock was more over the two-dollar price tag left on the picture frame than the return of the old painting. It's possible I'm biased.

Locke

DELILAH WATCHED IVAN PETROVICH step toward her on the pier made ghostly by the nighttime gloom. "Don't take it personally, Miss Samson," he said, broken nose still purple from where she'd punched him a week before. "It's not that we don't like you."

"A lot," his companion added. She'd never learned his name. His file was marked 'Snail' because he was always trailing the rest of the gang. "I'd get your autograph if you weren't handcuffed."

A freezing wind whipped the snow at her feet as Delilah smiled. "Take 'em off, big boy. I bet we can find a pen."

Snail stared, confusion clouding his round face.

Ivan shook his head in frustration. "No. You stay handcuffed, we stay alive. We've been over this."

"This is overkill," Delilah said as icy spray from Lake Michigan bit her ankle. If they pushed her in the water it would be merely waste disposal. With the arctic front that had moved in, all they needed to do to kill her was to leave her outside for another hour

"You're asking the wrong kinds of questions. Hanging with the wrong kind of people," Ivan said. "I bet your parents warned you about talking to strangers."

"Not as such, no." The shackles around her feet were making life difficult. Ivan had welded them shut before she woke from whatever drug they'd used to give her such a stupendous headache. If she wasn't careful, she was going to lose both her feet tonight. Or her life. She glanced over her shoulder at the water and tried to figure out if the heat from the broken shackles would be tempered enough by the chill of the water to escape with only third degree burns. Physics had never been her favorite subject. "I really think this is a bad plan, boys. If we go through with this, what will we have to do next time we meet? You're escalating the problem. All I want to know is what hit the street. I hate being left out."

Ivan grabbed the lapel of her woolen dress coat, pushing her back so she balanced on her Miu Miu heels. "You should have stayed out of it."

"Don't make me kill you, Ivan. You know what the dry cleaners charge. We go to the same place. Mr. Way is not going to be happy about this."

"But the boss will be. Goodnight, sweetheart." He moved to kiss her and Delilah kicked back, pulling him down into the water with her.

Cold wasn't the right word. Cold was

snowflakes, or iced tea, or the look in her mother's eyes when anyone mentioned Colorado. Lake Michigan in mid-December was a crypt. Death circled, numbing her to the bone. Water poured down her throat as she reflexively gasped for air. Be a mutant freak. Try to save the world. Die of drowning.

Heat burst around her as the shackles fell away. Maybe three seconds had passed. The freezing water had numbed her soul right out of her body. She could almost see herself in the dark water, feebly trying to claw to the surface but sinking anyway because her muscles couldn't move.

Mom is never going to forgive me for this.

The murky darkness of the water became an air-filled darkness bursting with pain. Cold limbs brought to warmth and burning from the change of temperature. Freezing water filled her mouth, her lungs... Air.

There was air! There was the sensation of someone holding her close, and then her knees slammed onto something too hard to be the muddy lake bottom.

Delilah choked, coughed, and vomited out polluted water onto a moonlight-smeared wood floor that bobbed up and down.

None of those words made sense. She made a living out of being sensible, politically aware, and biting her tongue. And yet the floor was bobbing at her. "Th-that's n' ri'." Her teeth chattered.

So unbearably cold. Pain. Cold. Heat. Darkness. Movement. She looked up at a shadow, searching for the man it belonged to—but there was no man. No light. Only a shadow. She forced her arms to hug herself for the relief it offered. "'Elp?"

"I can get you a blanket," the shadow said.

"'Es." Hot tears burned her face. She was alive.

Anger burst through the pain. Ivan was going to regret this night for the rest of his foreshortened life. She'd make sure of that.

Ivan. Snail. The mayor. In her mind she lined up the rogue's gallery. Dealing drugs out of rehab centers, now that took a twisty kind of mind. The city tried to reduce street crime by sending minor offenders to weekend rehabilitation instead of jail, and what did those hoodlums go home with? A nice duffle bag full of pamphlets, clean underwear, and dime bags of meth.

But something more was happening. The thriving Chicago sub-economy had gone quiet in the past few weeks, like birds before a storm. Or the jungle when an apex predator stalked past. She thought she'd finally caught a break when Ivan and Snail scheduled a meet down on West Wacker. All the evidence was on the camera... The camera!

She struggled to stand and started stripping off her wet clothes. If the camera was ruined... *Argh! Ivan you idiot, why couldn't you off me in the normal way?* His modus operandi was leaving people "drunk" and stripped in one of the parks. The cops logged it as a partygoer who'd wandered off and been killed by Chicago's infamous weather. It happened. It was a shame. No crime though. Why'd he have to change his style now?

Because you're a freak, she reminded herself. The usual drugs didn't affect her strange body chemistry.

"Um..." The man's voice was behind her. "I found a towel if you want... Should I leave?" he asked as she threw her shirt to the side and slid out of her pants.

Pocket. Fingers. Cold fingers never worked the way she wanted. Why couldn't the goons have been operating in Miami? This was it. This was definitely going to be her last winter in Chicago. In March she'd ask for the raise and a transfer to the Subrosa Securities offices somewhere warm. The French Riviera maybe. Or Spain. Or... somewhere. She wiggled out of her boots and dug her fingers into the lining where she'd slid the ultra-thin camera as soon as she'd realized someone was following her. *Hot dog!* With shaking hands she patted it dry. There. Good. Evidence. Now...

Her teeth started chattering again.

A warm, scratchy blanket was laid over her shoulders. Delilah looked down, saw a cord... followed the cord to a little green light.

"Heating blanket," the shadow said. He faded into the corner. "I know you're not a native, but we figure even tourists should know better than to swim in Lake Michigan in the middle of winter. That's why it's not posted on the docks next to the prominent 'Keep Out—Authorized Personnel Only' signs."

Delilah's fist clenched around the camera. "Th-thanks. Silly me." She sucked in cool air. "Where are we?"

"A boat."

Good. Locations were good. "Yours?"

"No."

"Mine?"

"Not that I'm aware of."

All right then. She nodded. "Phone?"

"I don't keep one on me. Makes me feel like I'm wearing a leash. It's good to get away from the day job, don't you think?"

She gave him her best *shut up* glare, perfected on her four siblings over the past two decades, and staggered toward a wall. Walls meant doors. Doors meant halls. Halls meant communications devices of some kind. Boats had phones, or computers, or radios, something like that. Her sum knowledge of boats was they were supposed to float, holes were bad, and boats talked to other boats. Ergo, help and warm clothes were just down the hall. And possibly up a flight of stairs.

"Where are you going?" the shadow asked.

"Help. Got to get help." She huffed on her cupped hands to keep them warm. There was a pop behind her as the heating blanket came unplugged from the hall. How inconvenient.

The shadow bent down and plugged it back in. "Sit down. I'll go find a phone. And some clothes."

A real gentleman would have offered his coat. Not that her mysterious rescuer seemed to have one. If he was who she was beginning to suspect he was, he didn't need one. Ghosts didn't need anything to keep the chill off.

Delilah sat on a vinyl bench and looked at the city skyline through a narrow rectangular window. Willis Tower was lit up for the holidays, bright, festive, and a beacon of hope north of her. So, 31st Street Harbor. Good. The cab could be here in a matter of minutes. She leaned back.

"Got a problem here," said the shadow as he entered the room. "The clothes are a bit big and these shoes..." He held up a pair of bright pink satin pumps in a lady's size twenty. Both her feet could have fit in one with room left over.

"Everyone needs a hobby." The words came out clearly between her chattering teeth. "Phone?"

"Nothing. I guess whoever comes here likes their privacy."

"Fine. I'll walk. Give me the clothes."

He held out a matching pink-sequined dress that was too big, bright, and cheap to ever be in her wardrobe.

"And here I thought I'd have to join the circus to wear something this tacky." At least the sleeves were long. Too long. Like an oversized sweater made in the middle of a sequin explosion. "Thanks for the lift. It was nice not seeing you. Enjoy your evening." She pulled the heating blanket's plug deliberately this time, folded the blanket neatly, and made a mental note to send one of the interns down to the docks with a small remuneration and the dress for the owner.

"Mind telling me what you were up to

tonight?" The shadow followed her down the creaky hall.

"Chasing bad guys, busting drug deals, getting evidence. You know, do-gooder stuff."

"You think you're a superhero?"

Ha. "Nope. You are though, right? The Spirit of Chicago, our city's favorite son. I saw the news segment you did in the graveyard last year. No record of birth, no name, no physical body, although you've just demonstrated your ability to lift things up, so I have to wonder how much of that was staged."

The shadows where his face should have been changed, shading to mimic the expression of a surprised man. "Says the woman who impersonates Harry Houdini as a Christmas Party trick." He sighed. "What's your name?"

"At home?"

The *Rosencrantz and Guildenstern* reference flew right over his head. "On your Company file."

"Locke." She smiled sweetly over her shoulder. "But I'm not listed as a superhero."

"The villain?" He swore so softly she would have missed it if she weren't expecting it.

"That's me."

"What are you doing chasing drug dealers? Did they cut you out of something?"

Delilah rolled her eyes. "No, I was chasing

them because you suck at your job. Your ability to catch actual criminals is matched only by your ability to stop time and speed up the harvest. You've never done anything but haunt people." She leaned against the rail. "Do you know what time it is?"

"Hot date?"

"No." Her date was lukewarm at best, and being stood up for the third time. Hopefully the mayor's right-hand man would get the point. Every time she ran into him, she fought the urge to stab his eyes out of spite. Alan Adale was the snake of Eden walking around in the body of a fallen angel. He had asked her if she was free for dinner tonight in front of people. There'd been no way to wiggle out of it without losing her standing. Besides, the local tabloids already had them pegged as Chicago's next Power Couple, as if that was something to be proud of. She was pretty sure Adale was up to his handsome neck in whatever was going down. "Time?"

"Quarter to eleven. You missed *Doctor Who*, but you should be able to catch a rerun of the *Firefly* reboot."

"Unlikely. I need to catch a plane. My intern is flying in," she elaborated when he tilted his head.

"Super villains have interns?"

"Well, superheroes have the whole side-kick thing pretty well wrapped up. I guess you could call him a minion, but since he's being paid instead of exploited, I went with intern." And if she missed his flight and left her sister's favorite student of all time stranded at O'Hare airport. Angela had doted on the boy even before he'd shot her in the arm. When he'd come to Angela's wedding over the summer, he'd mentioned he was having weird prem-onitions. Like called to like. Delilah'd ask some questions and, sure enough, Big Sis's favorite kid was a genetic freak too. His pow-ers were minor, premonitions of when people were going to die and the ability to heal a little faster than normal humans. It wasn't enough to win him a spot in The Company as a superhero, but it would be enough to earn him a visit from their silencing squad if they ever found out about him.

Delilah and Angela's family had closed ranks around the boy, herding him in like they had Angela's husband and brother-in-law. Travys was safe. And once he'd enrolled in the University of Chicago, she'd pulled a few strings to get him a place as her intern for a few months. It was the only way to train him to survive.

The shadow sauntered closer. "Where do you need to go? I can drop you off at home."

"I don't take boys home on the first date, or ghosts home ever. My ride will be here shortly."

An icy breeze fluttered her hair. Behind the shadow a man in a tight blue suit landed, face covered by a sculpted mask that horribly disfigured the handsome man beneath. "My ears are burning. Were you talking about me?" the man asked with a smile.

She could picture Ty raising an eyebrow behind his mask.

"Cute dress," her brother-in-law said. "Angela will be jealous."

"Long story. How'd you know I needed a ride?"

"Frederick called to tell us you were out of communication. I came out and waited. Who's the new boyfriend?"

"The Spirit of Chicago, and not my boyfriend." She walked over to her brother-in-law, waving careless fingers over her shoulder. "Toodles."

The shadow gave her a lazy salute. "Some other time, perhaps."

"Perhaps."

Ty moved fast, dropping her at the apartment and flying her to the airport once she'd changed. He hovered in the shadows. "You sure you're fine?"

"I'm perfect. No lingering affects except an abiding desire to get home and snuggle under my quilt with the heater turned up to eighty. Freddie is bringing the cab around. I'll drop Travys at his dorm room and go straight home. Which is where you should go," she added firmly. "Your home. Drop the camera off with Daddy on your way, please."

He laughed. "You need to go get your own errand boy."

"I have twelve minions and an intern who eats like a horse."

"Why don't you co-opt that shadow dude? He's here, why can't he work for us?"

Delilah smiled wryly. "Us being the good guys who fight the other good guys for a chance to fight the bad guys? There is no 'us', Ty. Maybe you and Angela have California tied up, but the Midwest isn't going to suddenly see the light and flee the strangling embrace of The Company. I'm not sure the Spirit of Chicago could. He's supposed to be the ghost of someone who died in the Chicago fire."

"He looked solid to me."

"Yeah." To her too. "I'll worry about it later. Kisses to Angela, tell Aaron I say hi."

"No more adventures before Christmas," Ty said. "Angela's been sleeping poorly enough as it is."

"Oh?" Delilah glanced up, although Ty's masked face gave no hints.

He shrugged. "Nightmares about what happened with Jacob. She wakes up screaming about fires. Not frequent, but between that and the stomach bug going around it's been a rough week."

She nodded. "No more adventures. Promise. I will not do anything thrilling, heroic, or risky for the next two weeks. Girl Scout's honor." A plane rumbled overhead, coming in to land. "That should be Travys. Have a good night." She smiled and walked into the lobby before Ty could remember she'd never been a Girl Scout.

The warm, stale air of the terminal was almost comforting. Still, she shivered. Nightmares were the bane of her existence. First her mother's memories of the time she was kidnapped and mind-raped in Colorado, and now her sister's memories of the man she couldn't save. She'd unlocked those, stolen them in unguarded moments, and they'd become part of her even though they weren't her experiences. A midnight swim in Lake Michigan just couldn't compete. So she tucked the fear out of the way, and moved forward. A super villain's work was never done.

Keep reading! Head to
www.inkprintpress.com/
lianabrooks/heroesandvillains/
to buy your copy now!

ABOUT THE AUTHOR

LIANA BROOKS writes science fiction in every form, from sprawling space operas romances (the *Fleet of Malik* series) to the antics of a super-powered family (the *Heroes and Villains* series).

Liana also maintains a soft spot for paranormal romances. She writes the popular *All I Want For Christmas* novellas, including *All I Want For Christmas Is A Werewolf* and *All I Want For Christmas Is A Reaper*.

You can learn more about her and her books at www.LianaBrooks.com.

INKLETS

Collect them all! Released on the 1st and 15th
of each month.

Dancer, Dreamer Seer

LIANA BROOKS

As Time Whirls Slowly Past

AMY LAURENS

Far More Satisfying Than Hell

AMY LAURENS

Just Another Day In Hell

LIANA BROOKS

Moon and Morning

AMY LAURENS

Some Impropriety Expected

AMY LAURENS

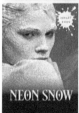

NEON SNOW

LIANA BROOKS

Reincarnation

LIANA BROOKS

More Than Mushrooms

AMY LAURENS

DOUBLE ISSUE

How To Make A Star & The World Ended

LIANA BROOKS

CAUGHT IN THE ACT

AMY LAURENS

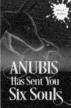

ANUBIS Has Sent You Six Souls

LIANA BROOKS

PRAYER TO A GODDESS

LIANA BROOKS

Love In The Time Of Corona

AMY LAURENS

RECRUITMENT

AMY LAURENS

IDENTITY Theft 101

LIANA BROOKS

Curses With Benefits

AMY LAURENS

NECROMANCER troubles

LIANA BROOKS